# TOOHY *and* WOOD

Other books by Mary Elise Monsell

*Crackle Creek*
*The Mysterious Cases of Mr. Pin*
*Mr. Pin: The Chocolate Files*
*Armadillo*

# TOOHY *and* WOOD

*by*

MARY ELISE MONSELL

*Illustrated by*

LESLIE TRYON


ATHENEUM 1992 New York

MAXWELL MACMILLAN CANADA
Toronto

MAXWELL MACMILLAN
INTERNATIONAL
New York Oxford Singapore Sydney

ATHENEUM
Macmillan Publishing Company
866 Third Avenue
New York, NY 10022

Maxwell Macmillan Canada, Inc.
1200 Eglinton Avenue East
Suite 200
Don Mills, Ontario M3C 3N1

Macmillan Publishing Company is part of the Maxwell Communication Group of Companies.

FIRST EDITION
Printed in the United States of America
10 9 8 7 6 5 4 3 2 1
The text of this book is set in Goudy Old Style.
The illustrations are rendered in pen and ink.
Book design by Black Angus Design Group

**Library of Congress Cataloging-in-Publication Data**

Monsell, Mary Elise.
Toohy and Wood / by Mary Elise Monsell; illustrated by Leslie Tryon.
p. cm.
Summary: After he loses his home and his friends in a fire, a fence lizard, who is also a gourmet cook, is taken in by a poetry-writing turtle who helps him deal with his loss.
ISBN 0-689-31721-2
[1. Lizards—Fiction. 2. Turtles—Fiction. 3. Grief—Fiction. 4. Friendship—Fiction.] I. Tryon, Leslie, ill. II. Title.
PZ7.M7626To 1992
[Fic]—dc20 91-38217

With so much love . . .

For Christian Giannini, your song plays inside forever. For my grandmother Elise, I know you are still here with me

# I.

# *The* FIELD

# Tomorrow We'll Worry If We Have To

Toohy sat on his fence, a lovely worn wood fence, and gazed across the field of moving grasses. He stretched his blue belly and watched the flies and gnats weave webs in the sky. He straightened his three-inch tail and pretended to be the fence.

It was a trick he learned as a young fence lizard. He was quite good at hiding himself this way. Black vees on his back soon looked just like grooves in the old fence. Even his friends sometimes had trouble finding him when he sat so still.

Toohy loved the fence. It had been there as long as he knew. When Toohy became an adult lizard, he had moved a few things into a house, under the fence, under the willows.

Toohy also liked to crawl along the fence to where the field dipped down to a grove of willow trees. There the trees grew into the hollow, their roots finding water even in dry spells from an underground stream.

It was a hot, dry sun that warmed Toohy's back as he lazed across the fence and told Bill and Henry about the next dinner he was going to cook for them. Bill and Henry were toads who lived in the soft, clay part of the field on the other side of the hill.

"Glazed beetle wings Provençal," Toohy began.

"Oh, I remember *that* dinner," said Bill. "It was one of your best."

"Mushroom-leek-acorn salad," the fence lizard went on.

"Good choice," said Bill.

"And . . . ," said Toohy victoriously. "After-dinner mints."

"Oh, yes!" said Bill, clapping. "Wonderful!"

"I don't know how you think of such things," Henry put in.

Just then, the willow branches fluttered above Toohy and the toads. It was Pearl, a beautiful gray dove who lived in the oldest willow. The tree was hollow mostly, and roomy enough for Pearl's house inside.

"Toohy!" called Pearl. She glided gracefully to the base of the fence, creating a great flurry of dust. Then the gray dove coughed into her wing and said, "I don't like it."

"Like what?" asked Toohy. "The menu?"

"Listen," said the dove. "I'm not interested in dinner at the moment."

"How about apricot-kale salad and mosquito mousse in a light pastry crust?" asked Toohy.

"It's not the dinner, Toohy," said Pearl.

"I hope you're coming," said Toohy. "I'm going to open up another tunnel just for you."

"It's the weather," said Pearl.

"You can change the menu, but you can't change the weather," said Bill. Henry laughed, rolled over on his back, and popped his eyes in appreciation.

"It's too dry," said Pearl.

"I remember when it rained," said Bill.

"Right," said Henry. "It was very muddy, wasn't it?"

"Great stuff," said Bill. "I miss mud."

"My house is cool," said Toohy to Pearl. "And there's plenty of water from the underground stream."

"We'd love to hear you play the violin," urged Bill.

"And read to us," said Toohy,

"Oh, that would be very nice," said Henry. "Better than our jokes."

"Right," said Bill. "Better than our jokes."

"I will come to dinner, of course," said Pearl. "But I'm worried. I don't like this heat. Not enough rain. Not enough bugs. And the field's too dry. It's dangerous."

"Dangerous," said Toohy surprised. "How can a field be dangerous?" But Pearl had already left, flying up to sit in the breezes outside her home in the willow. So Toohy turned to the two toads and said:

"Tomorrow we'll worry if we have to. Tonight, we'll eat." The dust-covered toads watched Toohy scamper down underground to his cool, mud-walled home to make the best of dinners for the best of friends.

# We'll Be Home When We're Together

Toohy cleaned his home and widened a path to his kitchen table for Pearl. By moving things out of an old rabbit tunnel where it arched high in a corner of his kitchen, Toohy was able to make room for a rush-and-willow chair especially for Pearl.

His house was small, but well stocked. He had a bookcase filled with jars of herbs, stones brought by the two toads, and books Pearl always left for him. There were all sorts of pots, pans, holders, openers, closers, emptyers, spoons, and every gadget one could make or find. There was a soft bed covered with pillows in the corner, three more rush chairs, candles in candlesticks, and a table where friends could sit while Toohy cooked.

He loved to cook. Toohy's kitchen always smelled like a field. Herbs hung from ceiling hooks in his kitchen and in the cluttered herb tunnel down near the underground stream. Often Toohy could hear the stream gurgle right along with the pots bubbling away on his stove.

That evening, Bill and Henry arrived first. They each carried a bag of small stones they had gathered for Toohy. He carefully added them to his collection on the shelf while the two toads settled into chairs and watched the delicious steam curl from Toohy's pots.

"A rolling toad gathers stones between his toes," said Bill. It was his first joke (or funny saying, as he called it) for the evening. Next Henry added his.

"What did one stone say to a toad?" asked Henry.

"I don't know," said Bill.

"I don't know either," said Henry. "I wasn't there." The two toads laughed together, so much so that their eyes bulged and they nearly fell onto the rush-matted floor.

Then they heard Pearl coming slowly down the tunnel, her long feathers brushing against the walls.

She carried her violin under one wing and several books under the other. Toohy stirred his pots and smiled happily while Pearl settled into the chair he had put in his kitchen just for her.

He had made the grandest of dinners. It began with dandelion gazpacho with dill, mushroom-leek salad, glazed beetle wings Provençal, and a special seed cake that was Pearl's favorite. As they all sat together at Toohy's table, the fence lizard scurried back and forth with fine-smelling dishes, then collected them again to pile high in a wide tin pan.

Once dinner was over and laughter from the toads' jokes faded, Pearl brought out her violin and played fast songs for dancing and skipping. The toads and the fence lizard danced while Pearl tapped her foot lightly, and the night went on and on.

"To friends, great dinners, and fences," toasted Toohy to everyone with his teacup.

"Right," said Bill holding his cup. "How lucky can a toad be to have so many friends to eat dinner with and laugh at his jokes."

Pearl raised the lustrous violin again from its blue velvet case and played a beautiful field song, one of their favorites. Everyone listened while the gray dove sang:

*Just a field full of song,*
*It's a song full of friends.*
*We'll be home when we're together.*
*Far from the field,*
*Remember its song.*
*Then you'll feel much better.*

Toohy, Bill, and Henry's eyes were full of tears as they thanked Pearl for her song. Toohy looked for a long, long time into the gray dove's eyes, then decided it was time for a fast skipping song to change the pace. So once again Pearl played and the three danced until the good friends collapsed into each others laps and onto shoulders, too tired to laugh or speak. The toads thanked Toohy for a wonderful evening and crawled sleepily out the front tunnel to a midnight moon.

Pearl slowly packed up her violin. This was the time Toohy loved most, when Pearl sat next to Toohy's bed and read to him until he fell asleep. Pearl would pat him gently on his nose and cover him up with a pale green blanket. Then she left the book right under his slender arms. It always happened this way, much because Toohy liked to pretend he had fallen asleep reading to himself.

"Tomorrow," said Toohy to Pearl, "I'll learn to

read. Tonight," he said, his eyes glazing into a dream, "I'll listen to you read and then I'll sleep."

So Pearl read gently to Toohy. Not much later she left, softly brushing the sides of the tunnel, her violin tucked under her wing.

# The Only Field I've Ever Known

It was well past dawn when Toohy came out of his home to sit on his fence in the dusty sunshine. It was so dry that summer that mosquitoes had become a delicacy and puddles were things to travel to. But Toohy felt a warmth and fullness that morning he would not feel again for a long, long time. It had been a wonderful dinner the night before, one of his best, with the most wonderful friends. He had decided to spend the rest of the day just thinking about how wonderful it all was.

It was in the middle of one of those wonderful

thoughts that Toohy suddenly was jolted right off his fence.

First it was the roar. But what scared Toohy the most was the wind fiercely rising out of the quiet. It shook the willows nearby, showering green leaves and twigs on his back as he sat stunned in the flattened grasses.

"Toohy!" shouted Pearl. She swooped down from the tree and landed next to him. "Are you all right?"

Toohy crouched low and shaking in the bent grasses. "I am *mostly* all right," he said.

"Oh, this is the big awful," groaned Bill. He was coming down the hill just as Toohy fell off the fence. "Say, that was a close shave," he said to Toohy.

"What is the big awful?" asked Toohy.

"Something dangerous. Very dangerous," said Bill.

"It's a storm," said Pearl, her voice straining in the wind. "It's a very big storm."

"How can a storm be that awful?" asked Toohy. He looked up at the fast-moving clouds darkening the sky.

"It's the smell," said Pearl, her voice straining in the wind. "Something is wrong."

"I smelled it too," said Bill. "Doesn't feel right."

"Where's Henry?" asked Toohy, worried.

"Right here," said the other toad climbing down the hill, hugging the ground as he went. The wind snarled and stung their eyes.

"What do you think it is?" Toohy asked Pearl.

"I don't really know," said Pearl to the fence lizard. "But I can see more from the top of the willow." Then the gray dove threw back her wings and bravely fought her way to the top of the old tree.

"There's too much wind," said Bill, worried, as he watched Pearl cling to the swaying top of the willow.

"It's a fire!" shouted Pearl to Toohy and the toads. They could barely hear her. "Lightning," she cried. "A tree is on fire! The grass is on fire too! . . . Escape!"

"I can't," Toohy shouted back.

"Have to!" returned the dove as the wind clipped her words.

Toohy looked at Bill and said, "I don't want to leave my fence. And this is the only field I've ever known. We can't let this happen to us, can we?"

"Oh, it can happen, but it'll be all right," said Bill. "We'll all leave for a while and then we'll come back, right Henry?"

"Right, let's go pack," said Henry.

"No time," said Bill. "We're going now." He led

Henry through the thick grasses and called over his shoulder to Toohy: "Come with us, Toohy. You have to leave now!"

"I can't," yelled Toohy back to the toads.

"We'll find a field together somewhere," cried Bill, disappearing through the grasses.

"This is the only field I want," said Toohy. He looked up into the willow. The wind stopped for a moment as if to gather strength. And in that quiet Toohy shouted to Pearl: "Will you come with me?"

"I'll try. . . ." It was the last Pearl said before the deafening roar and the crack that Toohy would never forget. It must have been the draft from the fire or else the storm that came up over the hill and, like a fist, shook the willow, ripping and splitting the branch Pearl clung to. It whipped wildly around the tree dashing Pearl suddenly to the ground where Toohy found her quiet and covered with willow leaves, her violin in its blue velvet case cradled unharmed in her wing. She must have saved it before she fell. Toohy swept twigs and leaves from her feathers and blew the dust away from her eyes. But the gentle gray dove just stared back without seeing. Pearl was dead.

Toohy curled his lip and shook with sadness. The rumble began again and the smell of fire was strong.

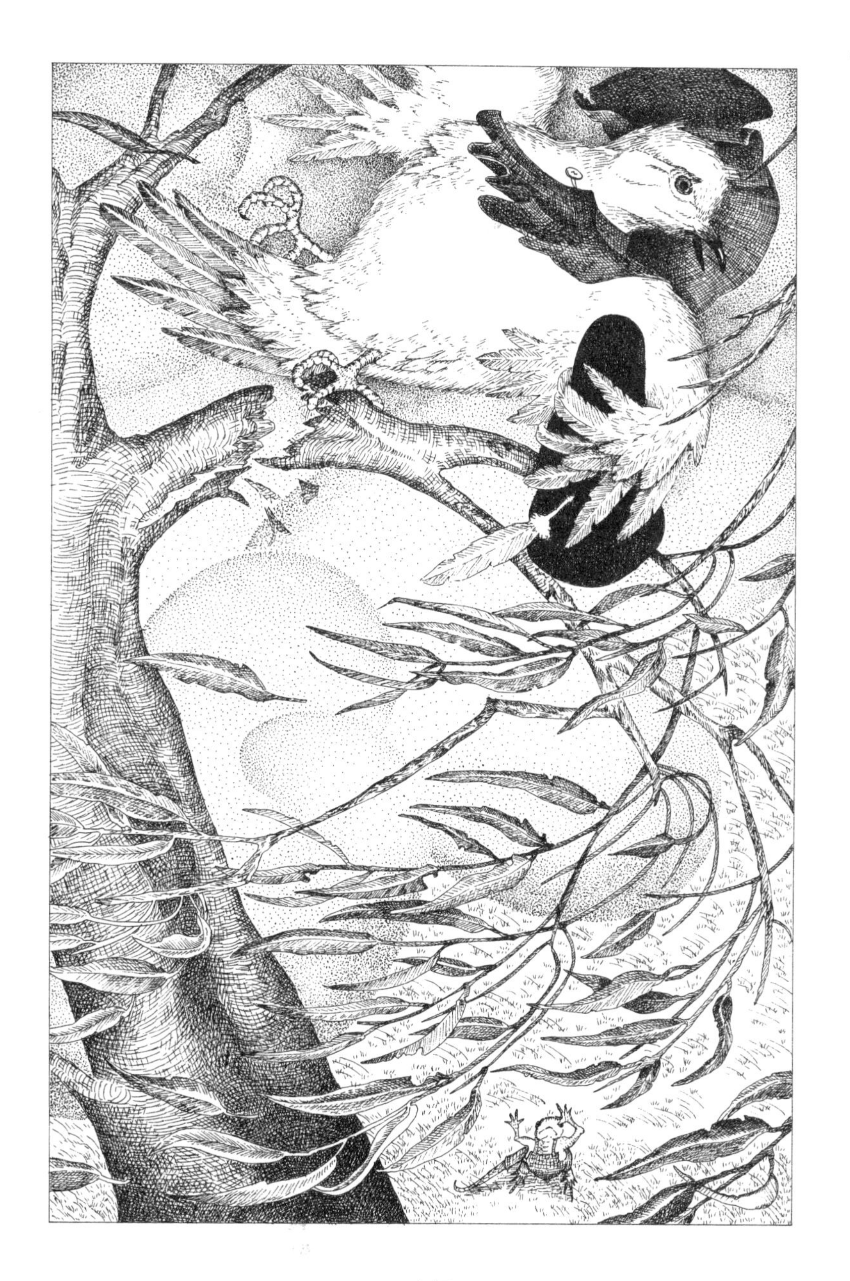

Toohy suddenly felt a sharp stab of pain. Another branch broke away and sliced off his tail. He would grow another, but at once he realized he would soon be in grave danger unless he did *something*.

Toohy closed Pearl's eyes then covered her with stones, small twigs, and green leaves. Then, aching, Toohy grabbed Pearl's violin and dived down into his home.

There was no time. Toohy was sure the fire would reach his fence and then his home. He quickly filled a small bag with a blanket, a few herbs, jars of food, and stones. Then he looked around his friendly, mud-walled home, sighing deeply when he saw his shining pots hanging by the stove. Then Toohy was startled by something he thought he would never see again. In the corner was a beautiful long gray feather. It was Pearl's. Toohy slipped it into the violin case, then started down the long, deep rabbit tunnel to the underground stream.

# The Moon

Toohy lit a lamp and made his way past his hanging herbs and jars of stones. The air became thinner here, but its coolness was calming to the frightened fence lizard. He climbed down and down as the sound of rushing water became louder and louder. Before long he stopped. There, wrapped in willow roots, was the underground stream winding through a long, dark tunnel.

It was an uncertain escape, but the only way out as far as Toohy knew. Above him, the wind-swept fire might have burned the entire field. Although he wasn't sure, he thought he might follow the stream to where it fed into a pond somewhere past the field.

Feeling along the tunnel wall, Toohy walked in the almost dark guided by his dim lamp and the sound of the stream. Suddenly he tripped right over a broken willow root, twisted and tangled in itself. Toohy held the lamp high and looked at the root closely. It was rumpled but sturdy, and appeared capable of holding a load. Toohy tugged the willow root slowly off the stream bank and set it lightly in the water, holding tightly to one end.

"Good," he assured himself. "No leaks." Toohy loaded his bag and gently set Pearl's violin case into the willow-root boat. With muffled rumbling and thundering overhead, he lowered himself in and shoved the boat away from the happiest place a fence lizard had ever known.

Although he had escaped, he didn't feel so clever. Mostly what Toohy felt was sad and awful. Maybe this is what Bill meant by the big awful, feeling all alone. It was a heavy feeling, as though there were a big bag of rocks in his boat with him instead of a few herbs, jars of food, and stones. He felt *so* heavy he thought he might actually sink. It might be safer, he decided, to feel awful and alone when he was on dry land.

So Toohy floated, his feet lower than his head, which was resting on Pearl's violin. The roof of his stream-cave was sometimes low, sometimes high. Eerie shadows of dark spiders flickered in the lamplight. Toohy didn't know how long he had been drifting in the dark tunnel. Maybe he had fallen asleep. He wasn't sure. Perhaps it was the next day or night outside. Just when he was about to think he might drift in his willow-root boat forever, the ceiling dipped very low. He heard a fast rush of water ahead. Before he knew it, Toohy was spinning around and around and going forward much faster. He held on dearly to the boat as he raced along. Toohy realized he was rushing toward what sounded like a waterfall! Toohy shut his eyes and held on tight. There was no stopping, no going back, and he certainly did not want to look.

Whoosh! It was a terrible torrent. Water sprayed his face and drenched his boat. He fell and fell and fell with the rushing and the roaring until he was sure he would drown with Pearl's violin and no one anywhere would ever know about it.

Then all at once he stopped. Toohy drew in a

deep breath. He opened his eyes. He was now floating gently in what seemed to be an underground pond, his boat drifting toward the wall of a large cave.

A few moments later Toohy ducked his head and skidded onto a sandy bank, just short of a sharp rock that screened the opening of the cave. Dazed and wobbly, the fence lizard looked around. Amazing, he thought. His lamp was still lit. No, he decided. It wasn't his lamp.

Toohy jumped out of his boat. There, peering like a face beyond the rock, was the moon.

"The moon!" shouted Toohy, the echo calling back. "Oh, it's the wonderful, old moon. At least you are still here." But where was Pearl's violin?

Toohy searched inside his boat. He found his bag, but the violin was gone! Then, under some gnarled twigs, he saw it. The case sparkled in the moonlight as though it had a song still in it. Toohy picked up Pearl's violin and hugged it to himself.

"It's still here too." Toohy told the moon.

The soggy fence lizard carefully pushed his bag and the violin through the narrow cave opening. Then he squeezed himself through too.

There he was outside in the moonlight among what looked like a lot of trees. Toohy thought he

would walk for a while until he found a fence. He needed a fence. He had lost his friends, his best friend. She was gone forever. But he could always find a fence. If the fence were large enough, it would be difficult to lose.

"A fence," he told the moon. "That's it. That's what I really need most." The moon darted between tall trees, seeming to keep up with Toohy as he walked.

The air smelled damp and sweet from a midnight rain. Toohy worried about night hunters and wished he were inside in his own warm bed.

"You are the only good thing in this whole awful day," he told the moon as he dashed between shadows. He had lost his friends. A brush fire had driven him from his field and his home. He had no idea where he was. There wasn't a fence in sight. He had even lost his tail in the storm, and he was exhausted. He looked up at the moon, which seemed to be listening to this whole tired talk.

He was so tired that the tears rolled down his face and sat in a puddle in his neck because they were too tired to go any farther. That was when Toohy decided he really needed a fence right away, and in a moment that is exactly what he thought he had found.

Bumping up against his nose was a lovely, worn, hard piece of wood. A fence! he thought. A good, solid, never-go-away fence. What a wonderful feeling. The exhausted fence lizard crawled to the top, breathed in the mossy wooded air, and fell asleep, his feet curled around his bag of herbs and his head resting on Pearl's violin.

# II.

# *Wood's* BAIT SHOP

# 5

# I'm Not a Fence, I'm a Bait Shop

Wood's Bait Shop was tucked into a small hill, just a short path up from Wood's Pond, which were all in Wood's Wood. Wood was a turtle. He was an old wood turtle with a rough shell, etched with many lines, on his back. He liked to write poetry late at night, often looking up at the moon for advice. Sometimes he would write very fast as though the moon had just given him the most wonderful idea he had ever heard.

This night Wood was writing a poem about turtle soup. Not that the moon had much to do with turtle soup, but it was good to look at when he was thinking about soup. Wood put down his pen and read out loud:

## Turtle Soup

*I am not very fond of that stuff you make.*
*It's dark and greenish and makes me shake.*
*Thinking about where you got what's in it,*
*Concerns a turtle who would not benefit from it.*

*In fact, turtle soup to a turtle is a very large threat,*
*About which no turtle is happy (at least those turtles I've met).*
*It's not a delicacy or tantalizer or appetizer.*
*Turtle soup cooks are just plain insensitively unwiser.*

Wood read his poem out loud a few times, scratching out this and that. "How about 'Turtle soup cooks are not very nicer'?" The moon seemed to nod as it drifted between branches.

"I wish I could just get that old moon down here to listen to my poems. I've written enough of them with him watching. I wonder if he knows what they're about. I think I have another poem just for you, old moon, from old Wood," said the turtle. He wrote for a few minutes and read to the open window:

*Are you listening, moon?*
*I have a thought for you.*
*Will you be watching*
*For when I'm through?*

*Are you listening, moon . . .*

Wood was about to start writing again when he heard something outside. For a moment he thought it might be the moon answering his poem, but the sound seemed to come from his own roof.

"Ahhhhh," went the sound. It was a little like a board creaking or the wind blowing in the trees. It could even be a snoring sound, he thought. Wood opened his oak door and walked slowly around his bait shop. A snoring shadow in the moonlight, Toohy slept soundly on Wood's roof.

"A fence lizard," snorted Wood. "What's that blasted thing doing on my roof? I'm not a fence, I'm a bait shop. Wood's Bait Shop, next to Wood's Pond, next to Wood's Wood." The turtle peered up at the fence lizard. He was small, he considered, and perhaps very young. He looked tired and muddy. Then Wood noticed Toohy's small bag rolled up between his feet and the violin case under his head. For one night, Wood decided, the fence lizard could sleep on his roof. But in the morning he would tell him to go and find a real fence to sleep on.

That was settled, thought Wood. But just as he started to go back into his house, his bait shop shingles started to shake. Annoyed, Wood looked again at the fence lizard snoring away on his roof. It wasn't the snoring that was doing the shaking. The fence lizard was shivering in his sleep.

"Acccch! Do you think I have a heart of mud?" grumbled the old turtle to the sleeping lizard. "So I suppose you'll be sleeping inside tonight." Reluctantly, Wood crawled up the steep hill to where his roof jutted out. He nuzzled Toohy once or twice, then eased him slowly onto his back. Toohy never woke up as Wood rumbled from the top of the hill, carried the fence lizard into his bait shop, and lowered him onto a warm bed behind a counter.

Even while he slept, Toohy looked lost. He curled into a small part of himself and seemed to disappear. Wood put the fence lizard's jars on a shelf next to the bed and tucked the violin under his arms. Then he noticed the pale green blanket spilling out

Bug Fishin
License
Sold here

of Toohy's bag. Gently, the old wood turtle covered the sleeping fence lizard with the blanket and said out loud: "I wonder . . . what will *ever* come of taking in a fence lizard?" With that, Wood blew out the candles in his shop and went to bed.

# Bug Teeth

The last Toohy had known, he had fallen asleep on a fence. Now he was inside somewhere staring at the backs of two rather large turtles, a squirrel wearing a fishing hat, and a mouse eating a jelly doughnut. There was the smell of sugar, along with a lot of clumping noises on a wood floor, and considerable talk about bug-fishing. No one seemed to know he was there and that was all right for Toohy. He really wasn't quite ready to have anyone see him. But he did wonder how he had gotten off the fence. Where was he now? And who had covered him with his own green blanket? He thought if he listened for a while, someone would have to say something about wherever he was.

"The best bug I ever caught was over by the cattails," said a wood turtle named Ralph. He was sitting at the counter, where Toohy couldn't quite see, talking to another turtle he later found out was named Wood. Wood sat behind a cash register ready to ring up sales. Next to Ralph sat a mouse named Vern and a brown squirrel named Filipo.

Beside the cash register was a domed plastic cake server filled with more doughnuts. Under the glass counter was an assortment of sugar cubes, chopped cookies, and various little pieces of cake. Each was labeled with a bug name: *cricket catchers, mosquito lures, dragonfly bait. . . .*

Hanging on the wall were fishing poles of different lengths, as well as fishing hats, sweatshirts, a shelf full of thermos bottles, and a sign that read: BUG-FISHING LICENSES SOLD HERE. There was another case filled with feather lures of all sorts, bug-catching nets, creels, and fishing lines. It was behind that counter that Toohy watched, with no one knowing he was there, except Wood.

"The best mosquitoes are in the weeds," said Vern.

"No," said Ralph. "They're better under the trees near the water lily."

"The white lily?" asked Filipo.

"Yes," said Ralph. "I caught a very large mosquito there yesterday. I had him in my net. He was squirming around, thrashing, buzzing, then all of a sudden zinnggg. Just like that, he flew away. Largest mosquito I ever saw."

"The largest mosquito I ever got on a line was as big as this doughnut," said Vern. He held up a long, sugary bismarck.

"I've never seen a mosquito that big," said Filipo.

"I didn't know mice like mosquitoes," said Ralph craning his neck out of his shell.

"It's not so much eating the mosquitoes," said Vern. "As it is catching them. I remember a time when old Wood here caught the Giant Mosquito. You see those teeth up there?" Vern was pointing to the cedar wall. Hanging just below the fishing license sign was another sign and a set of teeth mounted on a plaque. THESE TEETH ARE FROM THE GIANT MOSQUITO, LARGEST MOSQUITO EVER FOUND IN THESE WOODS.

"It wasn't so large," said Wood slowly polishing his counter.

"Large enough," said Vern. "Weighed close to two pounds. We had enough to eat for weeks. We would have had it stuffed, but all that was left were the teeth."

"They *are* large," said Filipo.

"Very large," said Ralph with respect.

"Now then," said Wood "what sort of bait will you need today?"

"Bag of doughnuts," said Filipo.

"Three sugar cubes," said Vern.

"Whatever you suggest," said Ralph. "And a roll of string."

"Right away," said Wood moving slowly. The cash register jingled merrily as he rang up sales. Then the bait shop became quiet as Wood waved goodbye to Ralph, who was off to the water lily to angle for another giant mosquito.

Wood knew a few things about fence lizards. He knew they sometimes didn't like to be seen, so very loudly he said, "I am leaving breakfast right here on the counter for you. And then I'm going to my writing desk."

Toohy moved slightly.

"No one is here except a wood turtle and he's just going to write a little poetry." Wood went on.

"And no fence lizard I've ever known was ever hurt by a turtle writing a poem."

Wood left a steaming bowl of oatmeal and raisins next to the cash register. Then he went to his writing desk. Toohy started to look over the counter and sniffed cautiously at the oatmeal.

"And no one I know has ever been hurt by a bowl of oatmeal with raisins," Wood called from his writing desk.

Startled, Toohy wanted to camouflage himself as a bowl of oatmeal. But at last he cleared his throat, peered over the top of the counter, and asked, "You write poetry?"

"Well, hello there," said Wood. "Yes, soon I will write poetry. You see, there is some thinking that happens before the writing part, and sometimes there is some talking. Sometimes I even talk to the moon. But today I see I am talking to a fence lizard. Not long from now, I am sure I will think of the right word and then I will write it down. By the way, would you like to hear my turtle soup poem?"

"Yes," said Toohy. "I like poetry. But can you tell me how I got here and where I am?"

"You were carried," explained the turtle, "on my back from my roof, which you can just walk onto from the top of the hill. Presently, you are inside my bait shop, which is set into the hill just up from Wood's Pond, which is in Wood's Wood. Now for my poem . . ."

"You mean I didn't actually find a fence?" asked Toohy.

"Of course not," said Wood. "I'm not a fence. I'm a bait shop."

"But I *need* a fence," said Toohy. "My field caught on fire. There was a terrible storm. I think two of my friends were blown away by the wind. And then I lost Pearl."

"Hmmm. A brush fire can be a sad thing," said Wood, stretching his long neck to listen.

"A tree branch fell and clipped my tail just as I was escaping. All I have left of my friends are a few stones from Bill and Henry, Pearl's violin, and a feather. So now I need a fence."

"Yes, I can understand a fence lizard wanting a fence," said Wood, rubbing the edge of his rough shell. "Was she a very good friend?" he asked.

"Yes," said Toohy looking into Wood's wrinkled eyes. "She was a very good friend. She could have escaped if she had flown away."

"Now, then," said Wood with some concern.

"It's all right that you escaped and you can stay here as long as you like. When you feel better you can look for a fence if that's what you really need. You can even use my roof for a fence in the meantime."

"Your roof isn't likely to go away, is it?" asked Toohy.

"No, I suppose not," said Wood.

"Then I will use a roof until I find a fence."

"Excellent," said Wood. "But now it's time for a poem. Would you like to read it?"

"I can't read," said Toohy.

"Can't read! Goodness. Then you can't write either!" shouted Wood, alarmed. "Why, that's sad. Very sad. Fence lizard, you need more than a fence. You need books, pencils, paper, words, words on paper, and speaking of which, here's my poem on turtle soup. What did you say your name was?"

"Toohy."

"I'm Wood and here's 'Turtle Soup.' Tomorrow, I'm going to start teaching you to read."

"Pearl would like that," said Toohy.

"Fence lizard," said Wood. "Someday, *you* will like that."

Wood read his poem while Toohy ate his oatmeal, and a little bit of the big awful feeling inside

Toohy went away. There was still a big space inside him, as large as the field he had lost. Maybe it couldn't be filled but just put away somewhere, like a jar without stones on a shelf.

# Toohy Looks for a Fence

Toohy stayed for days in Wood's Bait Shop, sleeping each night behind the counter, his head resting on Pearl's violin with his bag of herbs and jars of stones nearby. Every morning, Toohy went outside and sat with Pearl's violin on Wood's roof, watching dragonflies dart uphill from the pond. Sometimes he talked with Ralph, Filipo, and Vern as they bought fresh bait for their fishing trips. And sometimes he listened to Wood read poetry and go on and on about how fine and wonderful each letter in a word was.

"Now there's a fine letter for you," Wood often said. "Let me tell you all about the letter M."

Toohy listened patiently to Wood's story about each letter, but reading wasn't something Toohy could think about much right now. He didn't think much either about the dragonflies or the oatmeal Wood brought him every day. All he wanted was a fence, he told Wood. A fence was something to depend on. To sleep on. To think on. To catch bugs on. It couldn't go away. And *wanting* a fence didn't go away either. Nor did that big empty feeling that Toohy seemed to carry around with him.

So one day, when Wood was in the middle of talking about oatmeal and the letter O, he stopped suddenly and said: "Fence lizard, I think you should stop *thinking* about fences and go find one."

Toohy thought about that for a moment. It would mean leaving the roof, which was the closest thing to a fence that he knew of.

"You think I might actually find a fence?" said Toohy.

"Oh, you *might* find a fence," said Wood. Then the turtle wrinkled his old eyes and added, "And then again, you might find something else."

"But you say I might find a fence," Toohy insisted.

"You might," said Wood, slowly eating his own bowl of oatmeal.

"Where do you suggest I look?" asked Toohy.

"Well, of course there are many places for looking," said Wood.

"Are there any near the pond?" asked Toohy.

"The pond?" considered Wood. He scratched his rough shell and went on, "Now, let me think. Hmm. Oh, I think the pond might be a very good place to start looking for a fence."

"Then that is where I will start," said Toohy as he carefully tucked Pearl's violin under his arm and started to climb off the roof. "Today . . . ," he announced to himself, "is a fence day. A day to find a fence."

"Just remember, Toohy," said Wood. "The pond is very round."

"Very round," repeated Toohy as he started down the path that led to Wood's Pond.

"Wait," said Wood. The turtle scurried back into his bait shop and breathlessly returned to where Toohy stood a short way down the path. Wood handed Toohy a bucket full of moist cakes and said: "I hope this is the day you find *something* of your very own."

"Thank you," said Toohy. Then the fence lizard

turned and, carrying the bucket and Pearl's violin, walked down the path between the tall arched grasses that surrounded Wood's Pond.

As he walked, Toohy found some of the same plants that grew in his field and he discovered a few more that did not. It was a strange feeling to be walking about after sitting for so many days on Wood's roof. Toohy had not gone far when he heard a loud cry coming from the middle of the pond. He tumbled quickly down the hill and looked far out into the water. There in the middle were Filipo and Ralph sitting in a boat. Ralph was reeling in a large sand fly and yelling "Yahoo!"

"Quiet," said Filipo to Ralph. "You'll scare away the bugs."

"Can't scare away the bugs," said Ralph. "They don't scare."

"Then hold it down so I can read my book," said Filipo, warming his pelt in the sun. The squirrel wore a wide straw hat and had propped a large book in its shade. He read while Ralph fished for bugs.

"Filipo," said Ralph. "You ought to try this one. I'll just pan fry it with a little rice. You'll love it."

"I never eat bugs," said Filipo. "Pass me a doughnut, please."

"All right," said Ralph, popping his housefly

catch into a bug bucket that was slung over the side of the boat. He patted the bucket fondly, then searched for a doughnut. "Ah, here it is," he said as he handed a jelly doughnut to Filipo.

"Yo ho there," called Toohy.

"Hello there," called back Ralph. "Would you like to come fishing?"

"Oh, uh, yes," said Toohy. "But I really need a fence first. Have you seen any?"

"Ah, well . . ." Ralph rubbed his neck against his shell and thought for a moment. "Just the thing," he said. "It's not a fence. It's a house. But then again it *might* have a fence. Down the path and around the pond a bit. You'll see it when you reach the birch trees."

"I just want the fence part . . . ," said Toohy. "If it has one."

"Well, it is a nice little place with a stove and a few old pots and gadgets I think," said Ralph.

"But it might have a fence, you say," said Toohy, hopefully.

"Might," said Filipo. "My uncle used to store fishing poles there. Needs a little fixing up."

"I am really just looking for a fence," said Toohy.

"Suit yourself," said Ralph. "Nicest place around and close to the pond too. You could take a boat to Wood's in the morning and have a doughnut with us."

"Thank you," said Toohy. "But I don't want to sit on a doughnut. I want to sit on a fence."

"Can't sit on a fence forever," said Filipo.

"You can if you're a fence lizard," said Toohy.

"Yahoo!" yelped Ralph reeling in a moth. Toohy waved good-bye and went on amid the warm drone of cicadas and loud splashes coming from Wood's pond.

# A Round Pond

Toohy walked for some time through the grasses and wildflowers around the pond. He stopped to rest and nibbled on one of the cakes packed by Wood. The pond seemed much larger than he had expected. Actually it seemed more like a lake. A very, very large lake. And the more he walked, the bigger it got.

"This is a very long way to go looking for a fence," said Toohy out loud. "This may be too far for even a fence lizard to go for a fence."

"Yo, ho, over there," called a voice. It was Ralph from the middle of the pond.

Toohy traipsed through the weeds back to the pond to have a look.

"How are you doing?" asked Ralph.

"I'm still looking for the fence with a house," said Toohy.

"Well, it's good exercise," called Ralph.

"It's a very big pond," said Toohy.

"It is," said Ralph. "a very round pond too."

"And I'm getting very tired walking around it," said Toohy.

"Have you tried stopping?" asked Ralph. "Sometimes stopping helps being tired."

"Oh, thank you," sighed Toohy. "Yes, I have stopped. That's a good idea. A rest now and then does help."

"And sometimes," Ralph went on, stretching the wrinkles around one eye, "it is a good idea to look at things carefully. It helps the feet."

"Right," said Toohy, scrambling back up to the path. He sat down and looked around. Then he thought about how big the pond was and how long he had been walking around it. What was unusual was how much the pond seemed the same in a lot of places. He hadn't yet found the fence or the house Ralph had told him about. Maybe they had disappeared.

Toohy thought some more. If there wasn't a fence by the pond and he was very, very tired, perhaps it was just time to go back to Wood's Bait Shop. It was probably just too big a pond to go all the way around. But the question was, which way should he go: forward or backward? Toohy decided to go a little farther to see if the birch trees appeared soon. If he saw them, he would look for the fence. If he didn't, he would go back around the other way. In the meantime he would follow Ralph's advice and look at things carefully. Perhaps there was something he had missed.

What Toohy found as he walked around the pond a little farther was a sign nailed to a tree. Toohy froze. Signs were something to read. Toohy looked closely again at the sign. The first word was TOOHY. That was his name. Toohy started jumping up and down. He could hardly believe it. What a day. What a day, he thought. He had read his own name! Then Toohy looked again at the sign. Below his name were the words:

YOU ARE HALFWAY THERE

Happy now that he had listened to Wood's rambling on about letters, Toohy sounded them out slowly. "You are halfway there," he repeated. "I am halfway there!" he shouted. "I just read a sign that said I am halfway there. I must be halfway there."

Toohy walked on a little farther and came upon another sign. Toohy read out loud:

TOOHY, YOU ARE ALMOST THERE

"I am almost there!" he shrieked. If I am almost there, then I must not be very far from something that *is* there, he thought. What a great thing to be almost there. Toohy came to still another sign and read:

THIS IS A ROUND POND

"Wonderful!" shouted Toohy. "I have just read a sign about a round pond. But what does it mean? The signs say the pond is round, and I am almost all the way around it. Very soon I should find a birch tree and maybe a fence." Toohy thought his feet did not feel so heavy and pushed on. Then he saw another sign:

YOU ARE HALFWAY THERE

Very confusing, thought Toohy. If the signs were correct, he should be *there* by now, not *halfway there*.

He walked a little farther until he saw still another sign:

TOOHY, YOU ARE ALMOST THERE

Soon after that, the fence lizard spotted a sign that read:

THIS IS A ROUND POND

The more I walk, Toohy thought, the more halfway there and the more there I get. Then I get halfway again. Toohy was beginning to get very upset. Then, through the reeds, he saw old Wood standing in a clump of dandelions beneath two birch trees. Between the trees was the entrance to a house that seemed to go down underground. Wood was tacking up a sign on a wonderful old wood door:

TOOHY STOP NOW. YOU ARE HERE.

"I am here!" Toohy shouted. "Would you look at that. I am finally here."

"Have you had some good exercise?" asked Wood.

TOOHY
STOP NO
ARE

"Why, yes," Toohy replied. "I have. This is a very big pond to walk around looking for a fence."

"It is perhaps not so big a pond as it is round." said Wood.

"Yes," said Toohy, not sure of Wood's point.

"Did you find anything?" asked Wood.

"I found out I could read and now I have finally found a house with a fine wood door between two birch trees. But there's no fence."

"Do you think this is a nice house?" asked Wood.

"It doesn't matter," said Toohy to Wood. "I need a fence. Fences have fewer problems than houses."

"Would you like to look at the house?" asked Wood. He leaned against the worn wood door. "Inviting, isn't it?" said Wood, watching Toohy survey the outside of the house. "It could even be a nice home. That is, if you like it."

"But it isn't a fence," insisted Toohy. "It isn't even *like* a fence or the roof of your bait shop. Sometimes houses are a problem because you have to leave them, like friends you like very much. But a fence is something to depend on, so tomorrow, I will look for a fence." With that, Toohy turned back toward the path, waiting a minute for the turtle to follow, not sure he wanted to make his way back to the bait shop without Wood.

* * *

Late that night Wood sat at his writing desk. He looked up at the moon. "I feel a poem coming on," he told his round friend. And this is what he wrote:

*Toohy walked around the round, round pond.*
*He looked for a fence,*
*but what he found*
*Was that the pond was very big*
*and very round.*

# A Turtle Trap

The next morning, Toohy set out again very early to find a fence. He had a lunch packed by Wood, Pearl's violin under his arm, and his green blanket slung over his shoulder. Toohy had not been walking long when he heard out on the pond a loud "Yahoo!" It was lovely fall fishing weather and Ralph, Filipo, Vern, and Wood were all in the middle of the pond in two fishing boats with Vern paddling his boat in circles.

"Yo ho," yelled Toohy gaily.

"Yo ho," called back Ralph. "Have you found your fence yet?"

"No," said Toohy.

"You could come fishing with us," suggested Ralph.

"Thank you," said Toohy. "But I have decided to go somewhere else to find a fence."

"Sometimes it is good to go around things again before moving on," said Ralph.

"But not too many times," cautioned Filipo.

"Is that why Vern is going around in circles?" asked Toohy.

"Ah, well," explained Wood. "That's an old bug-catching trick. You see, one bug-catcher sits in a boat while someone else paddles around stirring up bugs. The bugs gather around the boat and then we catch them."

"*Sometimes* we catch them," corrected Ralph.

"Right," said Vern.

"Sometimes we just watch them swim around," said Filipo.

"And think about what it would be like to catch them," said Wood.

"Good luck," called Toohy from the bank as he continued along the path.

Toohy was having a good morning walk. Most of the time he walked and now and then he said, "Good morning." And the *good* thing about it was, he didn't have to say it *to* anyone. He could just say it to himself.

"Now, if only I had a fence," said Toohy to himself. "Then I'd be all right." And maybe more of that big empty feeling would go away.

So Toohy left the path around the pond and set out through the tall grasses toward the wood. Now and then he could hear a "Yahoo" from the pond, so he didn't really feel lost, just adventuresome. Once he had worried about night hunters. But at the moment, he was unafraid, almost hoping for something interesting to happen.

After many "Yahoo!"s and a number of his own "Good morning"s, Toohy realized that he was much farther from the pond than he had thought. In fact, he hadn't heard any more "Yahoo!"s in some time, just his own "Good morning"s. And then he realized it was much colder. The sky wasn't sunny anymore. In fact, it was full of dark clouds. He was just about to decide that it was time to go back to the pond when suddenly he walked right into something very hard. At first he thought it was a tree. But it was flat, worn thin in places, with a splinter here and there. He carefully felt with his nose and his tiny claws and at last with his grown-back tail. Then he felt again. It was too perfect to believe.

"A fence!" he cried. "A fence, a fence, a fence! I have found a fence! Oh, just look at this! Oh, what lovely wood. What wonderful grooves. Just the right size for a fence lizard. I think I'll stay here forever. I should tell old Wood that I won't be needing his roof. But first, I'll just stay on this fence for a little while."

Toohy climbed up onto the fence, which was sagging and overgrown with weeds. Parts of it wobbled and even fell as he climbed along a slanted rail. But it didn't matter to Toohy. He had his fence and that was all he he needed. He put Pearl's violin under his head and the pale green blanket over his back and thought about how wonderful his new fence was.

Toohy didn't notice the first few drops of rain. They didn't make his blanket very wet. And he thought he could pretend his nose was't very wet either. But after a while, he knew it was *really* beginning to rain quite hard, more than just a few drops here and there. Then the wind gathered up swirls of leaves and blew them about. The tall grass swayed back and forth. And that was when Toohy started to feel the storm become loud and fierce like the one in his field some time ago.

All of a sudden, there was a loud crackle of thunder. Toohy jumped to the ground shaking. Then there was more crackling and lightning flashed again and again. Toohy froze. If he pretended to be the fence, he thought, maybe it would just all go away.

But it did not go away, and he remembered losing the gentle gray dove in another storm. The big awful space inside him seemed to grow larger. Pressing against the fence, he cried: "Oh, Pearl, where are you? I miss you." It was the first time Toohy had said it.

But as Toohy wrapped his green blanket all around himself with Pearl's violin under his arm, he started to feel better. The violin had a warmth that helped him remember the gray dove's song. He could hear the dancing and skipping in his underground home and the books Pearl read as the night went on and on. And he remembered her soft breathing when she tucked him in.

"I told her I would learn to read," said Toohy out loud. "And that's what I did. I learned to read. It was Wood who taught me to read and gave me a roof to sleep on." Then Toohy thought about all of the days watching dragonflies, eating oatmeal, and learning about letters. The rain was soaking through Toohy's blanket and he started to shiver. Then all of a sudden the fence lizard shouted: "I need more than a fence! I need to to find Wood and my other friends!" Ralph, Filipo, Vern, and Wood could be in trouble. Very big trouble. Bug-fishing in a storm was dangerous. Had they made it off the pond? Were they all right?

There was no time to lose.

Toohy wrapped the green blanket around Pearl's violin and thrashed through the tall grass in the direction he thought led to the pond. Leaving the worn wood fence behind, he made his way as fast as he could, against the biting rain, trying very hard to remember where he had heard the last "Yahoo!"

"Cccrack!" went the thunder. The wind roared. Leaves fell about. Suddenly there was a terrible cry.

Toohy could barely move. In the thick of the grasses, he saw Wood. He looked very hurt with all but one foot held tightly inside his rough shell. It was an awful sight. One of Wood's feet was clamped tightly in an ugly turtle trap. Wood moaned and Toohy rushed over.

"Oh, dear," said Toohy, looking at the trap.

Wood was stiff with pain. "What creature could do such a thing?" asked Toohy.

"I don't know," said Wood. "But I am feeling awful."

Awful, thought Toohy. How many awful things could possibly happen? He had lost Pearl, his friends, and his home. Now this. It was another big awful. Toohy stroked Wood's head as he wondered whether he could help this new friend.

Toohy pulled twigs and leaves out of the trap as the old turtle began to shake. He wrapped his green blanket around Wood and put Pearl's violin under his head.

Toohy looked at the violin case and said: "Now, Pearl, what will I do?" Toohy thought about the beautiful gray feather inside the case and looked at the treacherous trap. Something, he thought. Pearl would tell him to do something. So that's what he would do, he told himself. Something.

"Don't worry, Wood," said Toohy. "We'll do something to get you out."

Toohy looked around and found a branch about the width of his tail. Carefully he pried a part of the trap open and slipped the branch between the teeth.

"That's something," said Toohy out loud.

He held Wood's leg with his own to protect it from the trap and pulled the teeth open slowly. The trap snapped. Toohy looked down. Wood was free! But the old turtle's eyes rolled back in his head.

"We have to get you home," said Toohy to Wood. The turtle didn't answer. Toohy could hear him breathing, but he worried that the bait shop was too far to take the injured turtle. Thunderheads filled the sky. Lightning zigzagged to the ground. Then Toohy saw through the grasses, not far ahead, a sign Wood had made:

TOOHY, YOU ARE ALMOST THERE

Toohy thought for a moment. "Yes. That's it! I must be almost there. I must be near the pond. And if I am near the pond, I must be near the house on the pond."

With that, Toohy gently rolled Wood over on his back, and slowly, very slowly, pushed him to the muddy path around the pond.

Toohy stopped now and then to wipe mud from the old turtle's eyes and to pat him gently on his shell. But Toohy didn't rest until he reached the house between the birch trees.

You
almost

There Toohy found the worn door unlocked, so he carefully eased Wood down a few steps to the coziest house he had ever seen. Once inside, he found a bed, a table, a few chairs, a stove, pots, pans, candles, and even a few openers and closers. Toohy helped Wood, who had mostly slept during the painful journey, onto the bed where he covered him with another blanket. Then he lit a candle and set about looking for a pot to make tea.

It was then that Toohy remembered the dandelions outside the house. He went out again in the storm to gather several in his pockets. He collected rainwater in a pot he had found and put it on to boil along with the dandelions. Then he wrapped several more dandelion leaves in a small blanket and put it on Wood's injured foot.

As soon as the tea was ready, Toohy spooned it into Wood's wrinkled mouth and covered him with more blankets he had found. He hung his green blanket on a chair to dry by the stove. After a while, Wood's soft brown color slowly returned as he snored loudly into the night.

Toohy sat for a while next to Wood, then hurried about fixing and cleaning the little house. He wasn't sure why he was doing it, but the more he did, the more he wanted to do. So by morning he was surprised to wake up sitting in a chair next to Wood in a tidy house with clean dishes and shining pots.

There was a knock on the door.

What a surprise. He wasn't even sure he was really in this little house. But here was someone else who already knew that he was.

Toohy opened his door, but what came in first was something rough and made of wood.

"A fence!" shouted Toohy. "Just look at that!"

"Where would you like all of this?" asked Ralph, who was carrying a small bundle of fence rails on his back. Ralph went on, "We found these rails this morning. Not far away. Must have fallen down in the storm. But we thought we could sort of put them all together and make a fence. No one seemed to really need them. We thought you might feel more at home if you had a fence."

"Yes," said Toohy. He looked more closely at the pieces of fence. They were indeed from the same one he had found the day before and here they were again! Toohy patted Ralph on his back and said: "It is wonderful that you are all right."

"Terrible storm," said Ralph.

"Scared the bugs," Filipo said, following closely behind Ralph. "We got off the pond right away."

"Bugs don't scare," put in Ralph. "Now, where

would you like, uh, this fence? In the kitchen?" He adjusted the heavy bundle on his large back.

"Isn't it wonderful?" Toohy went on, happily. "Wood is here, you are all right, and you have a fence. But where's Vern?"

"Right here," came a voice behind Ralph. Filipo and Vern had both helped Ralph with the fence. Vern ran around picking up pieces that had fallen off.

"How did you know I was here?" asked Toohy.

"Tracks," said Ralph. "And I thought you might have come here to get out of the storm. Wasn't expecting to see Wood here too. We saw him get off the pond when the lightning started. After that, we got worried when he wasn't in the bait shop this morning."

"May I suggest . . . ," came a rough voice from Wood in the corner, "that you put the fence somewhere outside."

"Outside," said Toohy, excitedly. "Yes, outside would be perfect. But not in front of the door. That would make it difficult for visitors when they come to dinner. Dinner, that's a good idea. Tonight, perhaps. Or later. I'm not sure. I'll need a few bugs and the herbs I left in the bait shop. Oh, what a day."

"It was quite a day yesterday," said Wood to the

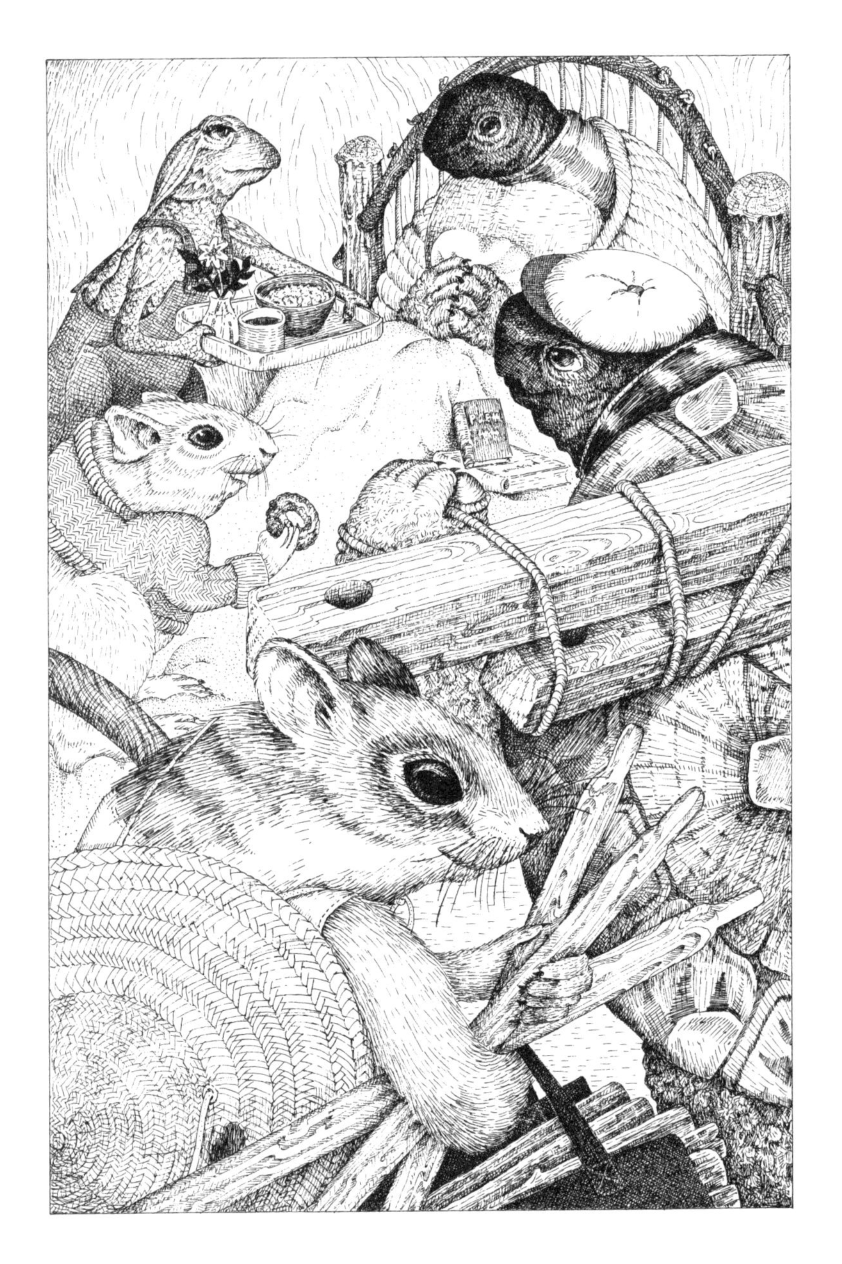

others, sitting up in bed. He told them all how Toohy had saved his life and brought him to the birch tree house in the middle of the storm.

"You are a brilliant fence lizard," said Filipo.

"Cheers to Toohy," said Vern.

"You saved old Wood," said Ralph. "By the way," he went on. "When we were out in another field, we talked to some toads named Henry and Bill. They said they knew you and said to say hello. They will come and visit now that they know where you are."

"Yes," said Toohy. "I am here. Oh, how wonderful it is to be here. Bill and Henry are all right. And you are all right. And old Wood is all right. What a great day to find out friends are all right. A very great day. A very splendid day. Thank you for everything."

That evening Toohy cooked a grand dinner in his new home: beetle wings Provençal, acorn-apricot salad, and a wonderful cake from Wood's Bait Shop. After dinner, everyone sat very quietly, Wood half-sleeping with a tray propped on the bed. Then all at once, the old turtle opened his eyes wide and cleared his throat.

"Ahem," Wood coughed. "I propose a toast."

"To bug-fishing," suggested Ralph, raising a glass of blackberry juice.

"To bug-catching," said Filipo.

"To friends," toasted Wood, "great dinners, and fences."

"To Pearl," was what Toohy said as one brave tear rolled down his face.

Late that night, when friends had left and Wood slept quietly in Toohy's bed under a pale green blanket, Toohy sat at his kitchen table, with the moon looking on, and wrote his first poem, a poem for Pearl.

*I have a song, a song that plays*
*inside forever.*
*Inside my song is you, your song with me*
*now and ever.*
*I thought I lost you in a field, by a willow tree.*
*Now when I wonder where you are,*
*You are a song inside of me.*

*—Toohy*